www.mascotbooks.com

The Real Story of Rumpelstiltskin

For more information, please contact:

Mascot Books
620 Herndon Parkway, Suite 320
Herndon, VA 20170
info@mascotbooks.com

Library of Congress Control Number: 2017919441

CPSIA Code: PRT0518A
ISBN-13: 978-1-68401-536-8

Printed in the United States

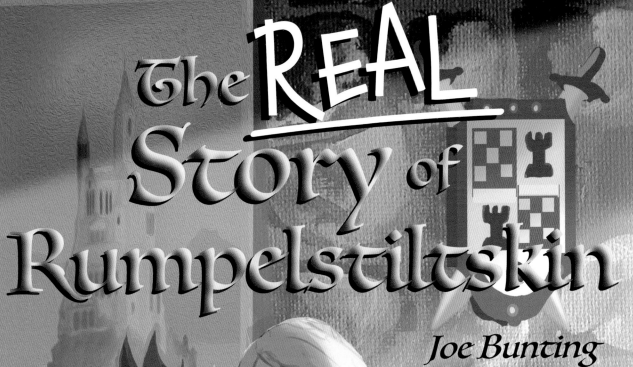

The REAL Story of Rumpelstiltskin

Joe Bunting

Illustrated by
Alejandro Echavez

My name is Rumpelstiltskin, but my friends call me Rump. I feel like I got a bad rap with this story of the Miller's daughter, and frankly, I want to get the REAL story straight.

This is how it really happened…

One beautiful July afternoon, I was taking a nice stroll through the countryside on my way to town when I passed a Miller and his daughter.

The King happened to be riding by at that same moment,

so I got off the road and hid in the bushes like the polite person I am. I overheard the Miller bragging about how his daughter can spin straw into gold. I specifically remember this because I thought, *That is so cool, I can spin straw into gold, too.*

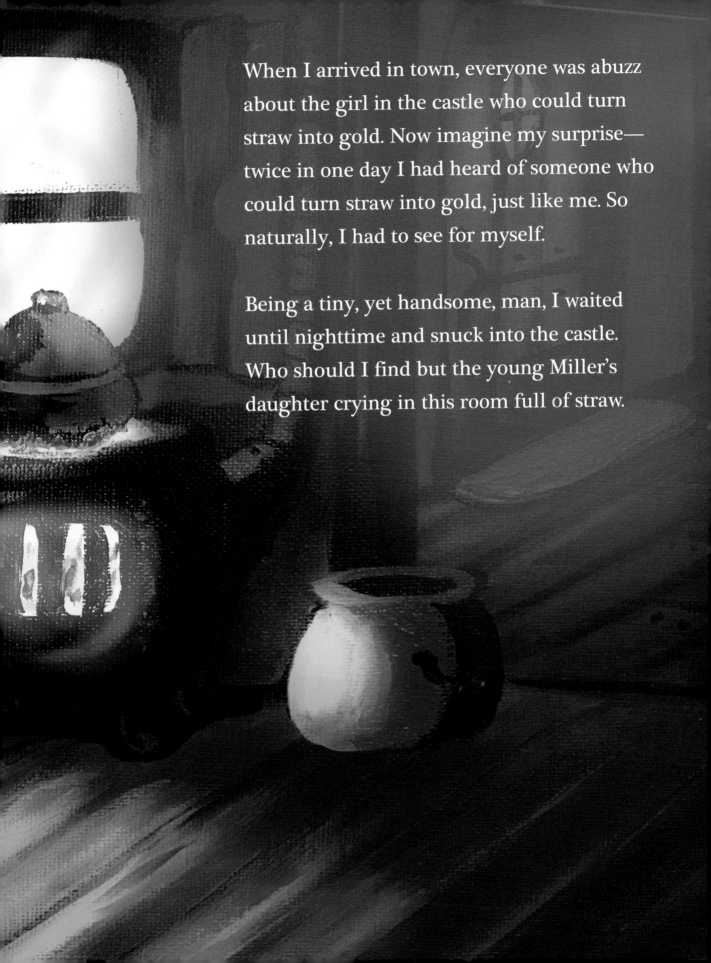

When I arrived in town, everyone was abuzz about the girl in the castle who could turn straw into gold. Now imagine my surprise—twice in one day I had heard of someone who could turn straw into gold, just like me. So naturally, I had to see for myself.

Being a tiny, yet handsome, man, I waited until nighttime and snuck into the castle. Who should I find but the young Miller's daughter crying in this room full of straw.

"Are you okay, my lady?" I asked.

"No!" she cried. "My father lied to the King and said I could spin straw into gold, but I don't know how. And now the King said that if I don't have all this straw spun into gold by morning, he is going to put me to death!"

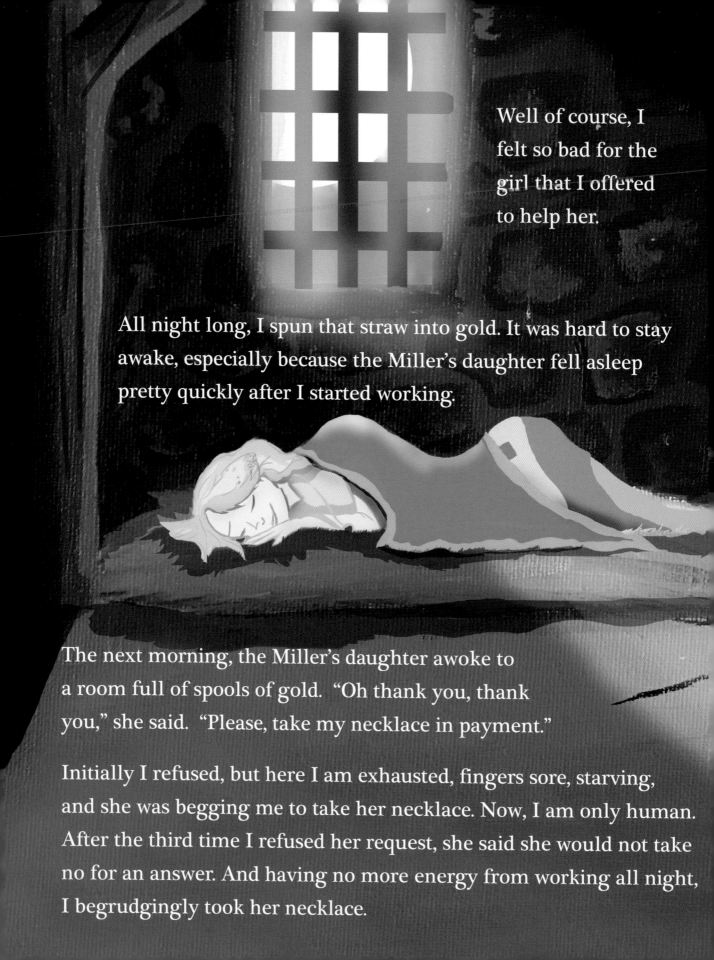

Well of course, I felt so bad for the girl that I offered to help her.

All night long, I spun that straw into gold. It was hard to stay awake, especially because the Miller's daughter fell asleep pretty quickly after I started working.

The next morning, the Miller's daughter awoke to a room full of spools of gold. "Oh thank you, thank you," she said. "Please, take my necklace in payment."

Initially I refused, but here I am exhausted, fingers sore, starving, and she was begging me to take her necklace. Now, I am only human. After the third time I refused her request, she said she would not take no for an answer. And having no more energy from working all night, I begrudgingly took her necklace.

When the King saw the room full of gold, his greed became even more intense. He led the girl to a much bigger room full of straw and demanded that she spin all of it into gold by morning or she would be put to death.

Now, I was leaving town that evening when I heard a woman crying from the castle. Being the gentleman that I am, I went up to see what was the matter. Once again, I found the Miller's daughter crying.

"My dear, why are you crying?" I asked.

"The King said I have to spin this straw into gold by morning or he will put me to death. Could you please do me another favor and spin this straw into gold and save my life?"

Now, being the caring man that I am, I could not sit by and let the King kill this adorable girl after she was abandoned by her father. So naturally, I agreed to help.

Once again, I worked all night spinning straw into gold. I asked her if she wanted to learn how, but all she wanted to do was sleep. *Seriously?* I thought, but I let it go. It was hard to concentrate with her snoring, but I got it done.

That morning, she awoke to find the room full of gold spools, and she begged me to take her ring as payment. This time I was not so quick to say no. After all, I had worked all night long with no rest and no snacks, and she had slept comfortably the whole time. You bet I am going to take some payment for my services.

When the king saw that all the straw had been spun into gold, he was once again overjoyed. He brought her to the largest room in the castle, which was full to the brim with straw. "If you spin this straw into gold as well, I will marry you and make you queen of all the land!" he proclaimed.

I was on my way out of town when I heard a woman crying again. I told myself not to get involved, but I have such a kind heart that I had to see. Not surprisingly, it was the Miller's daughter again.

"Are you kidding me?" I asked. "How are you still in this situation? You need to come clean with the King."

"He promised that if I spin this straw into gold he will make me his queen. Will you please just help me this last time?" she cried. "I will give you anything."

"But you don't have anything left to give me."

"I promise that when I am
queen you can have my firstborn child,"
she said.

Put yourself in my shoes. I'm thinking of this
poor defenseless unborn child. This poor baby's father
is a ruthless King who's threatening to kill the mother if she
doesn't do what he wants. How do you think he would treat
the baby? Not to mention the lazy mother who doesn't want to
work. How well would she take care of the baby? Don't even
get me started on the Miller for a grandfather.

I would be doing this baby a huge favor by raising it myself.
I'm a wonderful guy who's constantly helping people in
trouble. I have saved this woman's life numerous times
already. So I told her, "I accept your offer. I will spin this straw
into gold if you give me your firstborn."

"Agreed!" she said. We shook hands and the promise
was made.

The next morning, after I spun all the straw into gold, the King announced his engagement to the Miller's daughter. They were married that following night. The Miller never came, by the way. Just more proof that I'd raise this baby better than all these other people.

A year passed by and the queen had a beautiful baby boy. So naturally I came to collect my payment. Imagine my shock when the queen refused to give me the baby! Where I come from, a deal is a deal.

Now, I'm not going to kidnap the baby, even if it's rightfully mine.

I could tell she was emotional about this decision, so I made a deal with the queen that if she could guess my name within the next three days she could keep her baby.

To think all this time, she never even asked me my name. What kind of a person doesn't ask someone coming to their rescue their name? And you think she should be raising a child? Are we going to have a whole kingdom of non-name-askers?

On the first night, she tried every name in the kingdom. "Is it David? George? Mathew? Cayson?" To each one, I simply replied, "Nope, that is not my name."

On the second day, she started trying all the crazy names. "Is your name Adelbert? What about Brynjar? I know, I know, is it Zonko?" But I simply said, "Nope, that is not my name," to each one.

I went home to put some final touches on the nursery and practice my sweet lullaby for when the baby arrived. Well, the lullaby happened to have my name in it, and as I later learned, one of the Queen's servants had followed me home and overheard me! What kind of a person sneaks around outside someone's house at night, I ask you?

Well, off she went to the castle to tell the Queen.

For the record, children, that is cheating...

Anyway, that night I arrived at the castle and she began to guess all sorts of wild names. And just when I thought this baby was mine, she shouted out, "I know! It must be…Rumpelstiltskin!"

You can imagine my shock! How in the world did she guess my name? I mean seriously? In all the years I was in school, none of my teachers could even pronounce my name and now here the Queen just guessed it!! But I'm a man of my word, so I left without the baby. According to her version of the story, I said some bad words as I was leaving, but I doubt it. I was too shocked that the Queen managed to guess my name.

To my everlasting
surprise, I heard later
this crazy story about a little
man named Rumpelstiltskin
who greedily profited from the poor
Miller's daughter's situation. Taking
all her jewelry and then trying to steal
her baby to boot! Unbelievable! I am glad
you now know the REAL story of how it
happened. If you really think about it, I am
the hero of the story. Tell your friends.

About the Author

Joe Bunting is a new up and coming children's book author
with a playful way of capturing the attention of his readers.
As a father of two, Joe started writing stories to entertain and
captivate his young children at bedtime, which evolved into an
upcoming series of untold classic tales. Joe has a unique skill
for transforming classic tales and twisting your perspective of
what really happened. You never know where the story will
lead, but always enjoy the ride.